This book belongs to Nicole Faille + S[illegible]
+ Tyler Faille

Mole & Shrew

&ε; Jackie French Koller &ε;

illustrated by Stella Ormai

ATHENEUM   1991   NEW YORK

Collier Macmillan Canada
Toronto
Maxwell Macmillan International Publishing Group
New York   Oxford   Singapore   Sydney

Text copyright © 1991 by Jackie French Koller
Illustrations copyright © 1991 by Stella Ormai

Atheneum
Macmillan Publishing Company
866 Third Avenue
New York, NY 10022

Collier Macmillan Canada, Inc.
1200 Eglinton Avenue East
Suite 200
Don Mills, Ontario M3C 3N1

First edition
Printed in Hong Kong

1   2   3   4   5   6   7   8   9   10

Library of Congress Cataloging-in-Publication Data

Koller, Jackie French.
Mole and shrew/Jackie French Koller; illustrated by Stella
Ormai.—1st ed.
p.   cm.
Summary: When his relatives crowd Mole out of his house, Shrew
tries to find him another dwelling.
ISBN 0–689–31611–9
[1. Dwellings—Fiction.   2. Moles—Fiction.   3. Shrews—Fiction.]
I. Ormai, Stella, ill.   II. Title.
PZ7.K833Mo   1991
[E]—dc20
90-609   CIP   AC

To Kerri, whose smiles are like sunshine
—J. F. K.

For Maya Grace, with love
—S. O.

Shrew got up and got dressed. She walked sleepily into her bathroom and opened the door of her medicine cabinet. She blinked, rubbed her eyes, then slammed it shut again.

"There's a face in my cabinet!" she screamed.

"Help!" cried a muffled voice.

Shrew trembled. "Wh-who said that?" she asked.

"Me," said the voice.

"Me who?" asked Shrew.

"Me...Mole," said the voice.

"Why are you in my cabinet, Mole?" asked Shrew.

"I'm not quite sure," said Mole, sounding very forlorn.

Shrew opened the cabinet enough to see Mole's frightened eyes.

"What's wrong?" asked Shrew.

"I'm lost," said Mole.

"I should say so," said Shrew.

"Well, go ahead," said Mole.

"Go ahead and what?" asked Shrew.

"Go ahead and say so."

"I just did!"

"Oh," said Mole. "I really must listen more carefully."

Shrew opened the cabinet wider. "You appear to be stuck," she said.

"I am," said Mole, "but I think I can manage."

He wiggled and squirmed, and great piles of dirt fell out around him.

"You're making quite a mess," snapped Shrew.

"I'm sorry," said Mole, "but I burrowed my way in, you see, and burrowing *is* a messy business."

Suddenly Mole slid out, snout first, into the washbasin. And there he stayed.

"Are you going to come out from there?" asked Shrew.

"My thnout ith thtuck in the dwain," said Mole.

"Well!" said Shrew. "That is most inconvenient!"

"Perhapth if you could pull on my legth?" asked Mole.

"Oh, all right," said Shrew.

She gave one hard tug, and out popped Mole.

"Now," said Shrew, "please explain *how* you came to be in my cabinet."

"Well," said Mole, "it's a long story."

Shrew crossed her arms and waited.

"It all began with my aunt Phoebe," Mole went on.

"Your aunt Phoebe?"

"Yes," said Mole. "She came to visit, and I tried to make her comfortable."

"But you couldn't?" asked Shrew.

"Oh, yes I could," said Mole. "I could, indeed. I made her so comfortable that she never went home. She moved into my den. Then she invited her nephew Fred to move in, too. Fred has five children. They took over the parlor."

"Oh my," said Shrew.

"Then came poor old Uncle Mack. I had to give him my room. Uncle Mack can't climb stairs."

"But where did you go?" asked Shrew.

"I put a cot in the kitchen," said Mole, "until Cousin Louie arrived with his soccer team."

"Soccer team!"

"So I tried the bathroom," Mole continued, "but there was an awful lot of traffic in and out."

"I should imagine," said Shrew.

"Yes, you should," said Mole. "Imagining is fun."

"No," said Shrew, "I mean, I *do* imagine there was a lot of traffic."

"Oh yes," said Mole, "and that is why I'm here."

"You're looking for another bathroom?" said Shrew.

"No," said Mole. "I'm looking for another home." He peeked out of the bathroom door. "This is a very nice home," he said.

"Yes," said Shrew sharply. "This is *my* home."

"Oh," said Mole. "Well then, this is a very nice bathroom."

"I think," said Shrew firmly, "that you should leave."

"All right," said Mole sadly. He started to climb back up into the washbasin.

"Not that way!" cried Shrew. She showed Mole to the door.

"Good-bye," said Mole.

"Good-bye," said Shrew. "And good riddance," she added to herself as soon as he was gone. She made herself a cup of tea and sat down to drink it, when suddenly, *crack!* a hole appeared in the wall right over her fireplace. In its center was a black snout.

"Oh no," said Shrew.

"Oh dear," said Mole. "I think I'm lost again."

There was a thump and a bump and a crash, and Mole rolled out onto the hearth.

Shrew shook her head.

"Mole," she said, "I think I had better help you find a home."

After a light breakfast of tea and toast, Shrew took Mole house
hunting. She led him first to the old cave where Badger used to live.

Mole shook his head. "Too big," he said.

Next, Shrew took him to Squirrel's old nest in the pine tree.

"Too drafty," said Mole.

She took him to Snake's old crack in a rock.

"Too hard," said Mole.

SNAKE'S

She took him home for lunch.
"Just right," said Mole.
"Mole," said Shrew, "this is *my* house."
"Oh," said Mole.

After lunch, Shrew showed Mole Tree Toad's old home.

"Too small," said Mole.

And Otter's abandoned den.

"Too damp," said Mole.

And Owl's empty nest.

"Too *scary*," said Mole.

It was growing dark.

"Mole," said Shrew, "you are very hard to please."

Just then, Mole spied something.

"What is that?" he asked.

"Nothing," said Shrew.

"It looks like a hole," said Mole.

"I doubt it," said Shrew.

"It is!" shouted Mole. "I believe it's an old chipmunk den."

"It's too close," muttered Shrew.

"What did you say, Shrew?"

"Nothing," muttered Shrew.

"Why, it's perfect!" shouted Mole. "And, Shrew, look. Your home is right next door. We'll be neighbors!"

Shrew was silent.

The next morning, Shrew got up and started breakfast. She put on a pot of tea and poured some batter into a skillet.

A knock came on the door. It was Mole.

"Good morning, neighbor!" he shouted. "I wonder if I might borrow your hedge trimmers?"

"I suppose so," said Shrew. "They're in the shed."

"Thank you," said Mole. He sniffed the air. "Something smells very good."

"Hotcakes," said Shrew.

"Mmmm," said Mole, licking his lips. "I do love hotcakes."

Shrew sighed. "Mole," she said, "would you like some breakfast?"

"Why, Shrew," said Mole, "how kind of you to ask."

Later, when Shrew was fixing lunch, a knock came on the door again.

"Shrew," said Mole, "may I borrow a bucket?"

"Yes, go right ahead," said Shrew.

Mole stared at the stove. "Do I smell soup?" he asked.

Shrew nodded slowly.

"I would make some soup," said Mole wistfully, "if only I could find my pot."

Shrew sighed again. "Mole," she said, "won't you stay for lunch?"

That evening, Shrew had no sooner begun her dinner preparations when she heard another knock.

"Enough is enough!" she said to herself, untying her apron and flinging it aside. She stomped over to the door and pulled it open.

"Good evening, Shrew," said Mole. He handed her the bucket, filled with flowers.

"What's this?" asked Shrew.

"Good neighbors never return things empty," said Mole. "And here are your trimmers. They were a little dull, so I sharpened them."

"Why…thank you, Mole."

"It was the least I could do. Oh, and Shrew?"

"Yes, Mole?"

"Well, it's almost dinnertime, and…"

Shrew sighed. "Yes…Mole?"

"And I've prepared a special dinner, to celebrate my new home, and I wondered...would you join me?"

Shrew smiled. "Why, Mole," she said, "I should be delighted."

"Yes," said Mole, "you should. I'm a very good cook."

Shrew laughed. "I'm sure you are, Mole," she said, "and I'm beginning to think you're going to be a very good neighbor, too."